4/03

Storm of the Century

Adapted by Kimberly Weinberger

SCHOLASTIC INC.
New York   Toronto   London   Auckland   Sydney   Mexico City
New Delhi   Hong Kong   Buenos Aires

ISBN 0-439-41911-5

Illustrated by Bill Jankowski
Designed by Keirsten Geise

12 11 10 9 8 7 6 5 4 3 2   2 3 4 5 6 7/0
Printed in the U.S.A.
First printing, December 2002

™

What do you get when you have strong winds, blowing snow, and dangerous ice?

The Storm of the Century! Televisions everywhere spread the news.

This was a job for the Rescue Heroes Team.

Billy Blazes, Rocky Canyon, and Wendy Waters zoomed toward Canada in their jet.

Roger Houston spoke to them from the Space Station. "A train has gone off the tracks at the top of a mountain in Quebec," said Roger.

"We're on our way!"
said Billy Blazes.

Wendy knew that Billy had grown up in Quebec.
She also knew that he had not spoken with his
father in a while.

Billy did not want to talk about it. "We never let our feelings get in the way of doing our jobs," Billy said.

Billy, Rocky, and Wendy landed near an icy pond.

"It looks like a boy has fallen through the ice!" said Billy.

He saw a man trying to save the boy.
It was Billy's father!
    "You go on to the mountain," Billy told
Wendy and Rocky. "I'll take care of this."

Billy carefully crawled across the ice.
He pulled the boy to safety and wrapped
him in a warm blanket.

He turned to see his father walking away. "Where are you going?" Billy asked. "There's shelter at the base of the mountain."

"I'm fine," said Billy's father. "It's the boy who needs help right now."

Billy was worried about his father, but he had to save the boy first. He hurried to the mountain. He handed the boy to the rescue crew and climbed up the mountain's steep side.

"Is everything under control?" Billy asked when he reached the top. Wendy and Rocky were already there. Before they could answer, a mighty wind blew. One of the train cars slid toward the mountain's edge!

The people on the train were very scared. Billy, Wendy, and Rocky knew they had to get them out of the train and off the mountain.

Just then, a call came over the radio. Billy's father had fallen off a ridge! "Take care of these people," Billy told Wendy and Rocky. "I have to help my father!"

Billy headed toward the hyperjet. "Hang on, Dad!" he called. "I'm coming!"

Billy flew the hyperjet over the ridge and set the controls to fly without him. Then he lowered himself down on a rope and pulled his father to safety.

There was a strong wind and the jet landed with a bump. Billy saw that the radio was broken.

"We have no way to reach anybody," Billy said.
"We'll have to fix the system."
    Billy and his father worked to repair the radio.
"We work well as a team," said Billy.
    "I've always known that," his father answered.

Back at the mountain, Wendy and Rocky Canyon had helped everyone from the train. "We're almost done here," said Wendy. "Then we'll head out to help Billy." Suddenly, the mountain began to rumble.

"Oh, no!" Wendy shouted. A ton of snow
was heading right toward Billy's jet!

Wendy and Rocky started down the mountain to help Billy.
Before they could reach the bottom, Billy's jet blasted into the air.
"It's Billy!" Wendy cheered. "He's breaking through the snow."
Everyone clapped and whistled. Billy and his father were safe.

When the storm was over, Billy showed his father around the Command Center. Everyone was happy to see them together. They had made it through the Storm of the Century, stronger and closer than ever.